TOUGH TRUCKS
The Dump Truck

Written by Craig Robert Carey
Illustrated by Bill Alger and Keiron Ward

SCHOLASTIC INC.
New York Toronto London Auckland Sydney
Mexico City New Delhi Hong Kong Buenos Aires

W9-BEP-829

No part of this publication may be reproduced in whole or in part, or stored in a retrieval system, or transmitted in any form or by any means, electronic, mechanical, photocopying, recording, or otherwise, without written permission of the publisher. For information regarding permission, write to Scholastic Inc., Attention: Permissions Department, 557 Broadway, New York, NY 10012.

ISBN 0-439-48728-5

HASBRO and its logo and TONKA are trademarks of Hasbro and are used with permission. © 2003 Hasbro. All Rights Reserved.

Published by Scholastic Inc.
SCHOLASTIC and associated logos are trademarks and/or registered trademarks of Scholastic Inc.

10 9 8 7 6 5 4 3 2 1   03 04 05 06 07 08

Cover design by Maria Stasavage
Interior design by Bethany Dixon

Printed in the U.S.A.
First printing, August 2003

Dear Family Members:

Welcome to the TONKA Tough Trucks series! Your child will have the opportunity to learn more about how things work while improving reading skills. I know that kids like trucks because they are big and interesting. They also like big and interesting words like the ones in this book. TONKA truck books provide an introduction to nonfiction text—the kind of writing your child will meet in textbooks and even on the Internet. Here are suggestions for helping your child *before*, *during*, and *after* reading.

Before
- Look at the cover and pictures and have your child predict what the story is about.
- Be word watchers. Look for new and challenging vocabulary words and talk about what the words mean.

During
- Encourage your child to use phonics skills to sound out new words.
- Provide the word for your child, especially when it is a technical one, when more assistance is needed so that he or she does not struggle and the experience of reading with you is a positive one.

After
- Have your child keep lists of interesting and favorite words—there are so many choices in this book.
- Encourage your child to read the book over and over again. Brothers, sisters, grandparents, and even teddy bears make a great audience. Repeated readings develop confidence in young readers.
- Talk about the stories. Ask and answer questions.
- Visit a construction site and practice using new vocabulary words.

I do hope that you and your child enjoy the big trucks, big words, and big ideas in this book!

—Francie Alexander
Chief Academic Officer
Scholastic Education

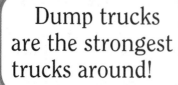

A dump truck carries everything in its bed. Who would want to sleep in THAT bed?

When dump trucks deliver their material, they dump it right off the truck.

And, of course, DUMPING is what they do BEST!

They use the blade to plow snow off the road!

Other dump trucks are short
enough to drive through tunnels.

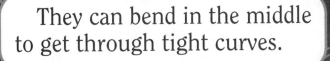

They can bend in the middle to get through tight curves.

Most dump trucks have ladders so the driver can climb into the cab.

The cab is where the driver sits.

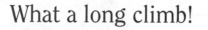

Some dump trucks are so big they have stairs instead!

What a long climb!

There is not enough room!

The really big dump trucks ride on a train or another special truck.

Here we are! Time for work!

This looks like a job for . . . the DUMP TRUCK!